Word List

Here is a list of words that might make it easier
to read this book. You'll find them in boldface
the first time they appear in the story.

assignments   uh-seyen-muhnts
adviser   uhd-veyez-er
research   REE-serch
librarian   leye-BRAIR-ee-uhn
Anthony   AN-thun-nee
Elizabeth Cady   i-LI-zuh-beth KAY-dee
opportunities   o-per-TOO-nuh-tees
microfilm   MEYE-kruh-film
issue   I-shoo
customers   KUHS-tuh-mers
advertisement   ad-ver-TEYEZ-ment
Bustles   BUH-suhls
suffrage   SUH-frij
Principle   PRIN-suh-puhl
ridiculous   ruh-DI-kyuh-luhs
quoted   KWOH-tid

Barbie™

The Front Window

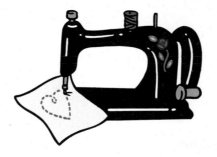

Published by Grolier Books, a division of Grolier Enterprises, Inc. Story by Claire Jordan and Della Foster. Photo crew: Bill Kroll, Mary Hirahara, Dave Bateman, Susan Cracraft, Mark Adams, Lisa Collins, and Judy Tsuno. Journal photography by White Light Studios. Susan B. Anthony's *The Revolution* © The New-York Historical Society. #54190 Produced by Bumpy Slide Books. Printed in the United States of America.
ISBN: 0-7172-8962-1

GROLIER
B O O K S

Chapter One

Tap, Tap, Tap. Skipper sat at a desk tapping her pencil. The sound echoed in the empty high school classroom. She was waiting for the rest of the newspaper staff to arrive. It was Friday, the day the high school reporters were given their weekend **assignments.**

Becky, the paper's **adviser,** entered the classroom. She greeted Skipper and rolled over to her desk. She grabbed her briefcase from behind her wheelchair and pulled out a folder. As the paper's adviser, Becky would receive tickets for exciting events in town. Skipper had heard that Becky had gotten tickets for the 'N Pink rock concert this weekend. She hoped she would get to cover it.

A few minutes later, the other students hurried into the room and sat down. Then Becky started the meeting. "We have two very different events this weekend," she said. "'N Pink will be playing on Saturday night. And tonight there will be a speech on women in the news business."

Skipper looked down at her notebook so Becky wouldn't see her frown. "Women in the news business" sounded extremely boring.

Becky tapped the passes in her hand. "Kevin," she said, "I'd like you to go to the 'N Pink concert and write the story."

Kevin looked thrilled.

Becky slid the other pass over to Skipper. "Skipper, I'd like you to go to tonight's speech and write your story. The rest of you have the weekend off."

Becky moved her wheelchair away from the table. "Skipper and Kevin, I'll need your stories by Monday."

"But—" Skipper began.

"Yes?" Becky asked.

Skipper wanted to say, "I don't want this assignment!" Instead she asked, "Isn't this old news? There are lots of women in the news business already. Just look at this school's paper. Most of our reporters are girls."

"That's why I gave you the assignment, Skipper," Becky replied. "If it feels like old news to you, find a new way to look at the story. Remember, do your **research.** Know your topic. Then write your story."

After the meeting was over, everyone said good-bye to Becky and left.

"I guess I'll head over to the library," Skipper sighed to herself. "Now *there's* a fun way to kick off the weekend!"

When Skipper reached the library, she went to the information desk. She told the **librarian** about her assignment. "I don't even know where to start," Skipper admitted.

"Why don't you start with Susan B. **Anthony**?" the helpful woman suggested.

"Susan B. Anthony?" Skipper repeated. Skipper knew that Susan B. Anthony had tried to get women the right to vote during the 1800s. But she didn't see what that had to do with newspapers.

The librarian talked as they walked into another room. "Susan B. Anthony started one of the first women-owned newspapers with her friend **Elizabeth Cady** Stanton. The two believed that men and women should be allowed the same **opportunities.** And the women needed a way to tell others. They called their paper *The Revolution.* To raise money for the paper, Miss Anthony traveled around the country giving speeches in the late 1800s."

The librarian slid open a drawer and pulled out two small reels of film. "In fact, Miss Anthony even came to speak in our town."

"Here?" the high schooler asked. Now *that* was interesting. Skipper sat down at a machine with a large screen used for reading **microfilm** reels.

The librarian showed Skipper how to wind the first reel of film onto the machine. "This may not be as high-tech as the Internet," the librarian said, "but it's the only record we have of such old newspapers. The real newspaper would be too fragile to handle. I'm sure you'll find a story about Susan B. Anthony's visit in these reels."

Skipper noticed that the reels were for two different newspapers. One was for their local paper *The Globe.* The other was marked *The Front Window.*

"That's strange," said Skipper. "I didn't know our town had two papers."

"Yes, we did," replied the librarian. "*The Front Window* lasted only a few years. I believe it was started due to a disagreement with *The Globe.*"

"A fight?" asked Skipper, curious. "What was it about?"

The librarian smiled. "I believe it had something to do with Susan B. Anthony's visit. I'd love to stay and research it with you. But I should get back to the reference desk. Let me know if you need any more help."

"Thanks," Skipper replied.

The librarian had set up *The Globe* newspaper on one microfilm reader. Skipper set up *The Front Window* on another machine.

Skipper sat in front of the glowing screens. She searched through every **issue** of *The Globe* the librarian had given her. But there was no mention of Susan B. Anthony anywhere. Skipper chewed on her pencil. "Maybe the librarian was wrong," she thought.

Then Skipper turned to the other microfilm machine and began to read. The very first issue of *The Front Window* was about Susan B. Anthony's visit. In fact, that was the only story in the paper! Skipper soon learned that *The Front Window* had been started because *The Globe* had refused to write about Miss Anthony's visit.

"So that's why I couldn't find any mention of it in *The Globe*," Skipper said out loud. Then Skipper remembered something from a story in *The Globe*. She quickly started searching it again. Finally she found the story titled "Storefront News: Don't Read It!" Next to the story was a drawing of a dress shop with a newspaper in its window. The artist had drawn a large X over the front door of the shop. The story talked about a local shop owner whose small paper was causing trouble in town. The shop owner was a woman.

Skipper checked the names of both papers' editors. *The Globe*'s editor in chief was a man. *The Front Window*'s editor in chief was the dress shop owner.

"Hmmm," Skipper said, sitting back. "This must have been the start of the fight that the librarian mentioned. I wonder what happened."

Feeling like a detective, Skipper began looking back and forth between *The Globe* and *The Front Window.* She read letters and articles in each of them. Slowly pieces of the hundred-year-old puzzle began to fit together.

In the quiet, dimly lit room, Skipper put her chin on her hands and closed her eyes. She began to imagine what life must have been like for that woman editor back in the 1870s. Soon Skipper found herself getting very sleepy . . .

*****

Chapter Two

Skipper lifted the full skirt of her long dress and stepped carefully along Main Street. She didn't want it to drag along the dusty road. Her older sister, Barbie, had just finished the dress yesterday. She had asked Skipper to wear it in the dress shoppe today so their **customers** could see it. "Wearing our dresses is the best **advertisement** we could have," Barbie had said.

After a horse and wagon passed by, Skipper hurried across the dirt road. As she reached the shoppe, she glanced in the window. Barbie always put her best dress on display. To Skipper's

surprise, there was also a sign in the front window. It said that a woman named Susan B. Anthony would be speaking in town that night. The sign hadn't been there the night before.

"Barbie!" Skipper called through the door. "Someone put a sign in our window!"

Barbie stepped outside and smiled. "Do you like it? I put it up this morning. A woman came in and asked if I would place the sign in our window. She had asked the owner of the General Store, but he had said no. The woman had also asked Mr. Sims at *The Globe* if he would print a notice about the speech. But he had said no, too."

Skipper frowned as she went inside. She was surprised that her sister would hang a sign that others didn't want in their store or newspaper. Reaching for the latest copy of *Godey's Lady's Book and Magazine,* Skipper studied the pictures of the fashion pages. **Bustles** were getting bigger. The fashionable pads were a bit uncomfortable to sit on. But they did give the back of a dress a nice puff. Skipper set up her sketch pad. Looking at the magazine's styles, she began to draw. Barbie's customers liked Skipper's ideas. They had ordered quite a few of her dresses.

Bustle

As Skipper settled down to work, the bell on the front door jingled. Mr. Sims stepped into the shoppe. As always, his hands were stained with fresh ink from his newspaper. And as always, he seemed to be in a rush. He hadn't even put on his suit jacket to visit them.

"Miss Roberts," the newspaper editor said to Barbie, "I saw a sign in your window next to one of your dresses. I hope that troublemaker didn't scare you into displaying that sign. I can take it down, if you'd like. It's spoiling your lovely display."

Barbie stood up and smoothed the front

of her cotton work dress. She shook her head. "Thank you for the kind offer, Mr. Sims. The decision to put the sign in the window was mine. And I plan to leave it there."

Barbie turned toward a neat stack of the signs on a table near the door. Holding one out to Mr. Sims, she asked, "Would you like one? It would give you information for *The Globe*'s story on Miss Anthony's speech."

"Who said *The Globe* would report on the speech? Miss Anthony and her friends are trouble. Watch out for them, Miss Roberts! I'm warning you." Mr. Sims turned and slammed the door on his way out.

Barbie smiled as she set down the sign.

"Aren't you scared?" Skipper asked, concerned. "If Miss Anthony is trouble . . ."

"Skipper," broke in Barbie, "Miss Anthony is not trouble. It's just that some people disagree with her ideas."

Skipper tried to remember what she had heard about the woman from New York. "Miss Anthony believes in a woman's suffering, right?"

Barbie chuckled. "I think you mean *woman suffrage. Suffrage* simply means the right to vote. Miss Anthony believes that women should have a say in things that affect them. Would you like to go with me to hear her speech tonight?"

That surprised Skipper even more. "Oh, I don't know," she stammered.

"Why don't you think about it?" Barbie suggested. Then she handed Skipper an old book. "Here. This was written by an Englishwoman named Mary Wollstonecraft a long time ago. She was one of the first to speak out for women's rights." Skipper began looking through the book.

But the dress shoppe soon became busy. Every woman who came in had something to say about Miss Anthony. Some liked her ideas. Others seemed to agree with Mrs. Steele, one of Barbie's longtime customers. Mrs. Steele said that voting was men's business. A woman's place was in the home.

Mrs. Steele was a no-nonsense customer. She kept her iron gray hair in a tight bun. She didn't like any decorations on her dresses, either. "No lace or ruffles for me," she often said. Only once had Skipper talked her into a navy blue ribbon on a gray dress. Gray and blue were the only colors Mrs. Steele wore.

"This is hogwash!" Mrs. Steele grumbled on her way out that day. "Miss Anthony should find a better way to spend her time."

But Skipper noticed other women taking copies of the sign with them. "Barbie," Skipper said at the end of the day, "I want to go tonight. I want to hear what Miss Anthony has to say."

At six o'clock, Barbie put the Closed sign in the door. Then she climbed into the front window and began taking the elegant burgundy-

and-green-striped dress off the dressmaker's dummy.

"Why are you taking down our display?" Skipper asked her sister. "Did someone buy the dress?"

"No," Barbie replied. "I've decided to wear it to the speech. I think this will be a night to remember."

Miss Anthony's speech was held in a drafty barn at the edge of town. When Barbie and Skipper arrived, they saw a crowd outside.

"It looks like a lot of people saw your sign," Skipper said, turning to Barbie.

But Barbie was frowning. Skipper quickly understood why. The people in the crowd were shouting and booing at women as they walked into the building. Barbie took Skipper's arm. "Just look straight ahead," Barbie told her. "And keep walking until we're inside."

"Go back to your kitchens where you belong!" yelled one man.

"And tell that troublemaker to go home!"
a woman shouted.

Skipper couldn't believe how angry people were. She wondered if Mr. Sims was in the crowd. But she didn't look around to find out. Once inside the building, Skipper could still hear shouts from outside. Oil lamps lined the walls. A small stage stood at one end of the barn. Skipper shivered, partly from nervousness and partly from the cold. Just as she was about to ask her sister if they could leave, the door opened.

Skipper turned and saw a tall, slim woman enter. Her graying brown hair was pulled back from her face. On her nose was a pair of small, round glasses. She didn't seem at all bothered by the noise. She just smiled at the small audience and took her place at the front of the room. Once Miss Anthony started speaking, Skipper forgot about the noise outside and the cold.

Susan B. Anthony talked about a woman's

life in the 1870s. In most states, when a woman was married, everything she owned, including herself, belonged to her husband. Women were forbidden to have careers as doctors, lawyers, or judges. Miss Anthony said that women all over the world deserve to make decisions for themselves. That was why women needed the right to vote.

After the speech had ended, Barbie picked up a copy of Miss Anthony's newspaper, *The Revolution*. Barbie read the words on the top of the page, "**Principle, Not Policy: Justice, Not Favors.**"

Skipper could see why people were so angry with Miss Anthony. Her words were powerful. But they made more sense than anything Skipper had ever heard. Never before had Skipper heard anyone question the ways of the world. Men had made the rules, and that was that. "Barbie," Skipper asked, "do you think Miss Anthony would mind if I took a copy of her paper?"

"Please help yourself," said a familiar voice behind her.

Skipper spun around. It was Susan B. Anthony! Skipper suddenly felt shy. "Oh, no thank you," she replied.

Miss Anthony picked up a paper and handed it to Skipper. "Just promise me you'll pass it on when you've finished reading it."

"Thank you. I will!" Skipper promised.

Skipper proudly tucked the paper under her arm as she and Barbie left the building. There were fewer people outside now, but Barbie and Skipper saw Mr. Sims.

"Maybe he is going to report on this after all," Skipper whispered.

"I hope so," Barbie replied.

That Thursday, *The Globe* came out. But there was nothing in it about Susan B. Anthony. Nothing at all.

Chapter Three

Barbie frowned and flipped through the morning paper again. "How can anyone call this a newspaper? Even if you don't like what Miss Anthony says, her visit is still news."

Skipper looked up from her sketch pad. "Mr. Sims was very upset by her visit," Skipper reminded her sister softly. Turning the page on her sketch pad, Skipper began a new design.

Barbie set the newspaper down and looked out the window. "But he didn't even listen to her speech. People should know about Miss Anthony's ideas. Then they can decide for themselves whether or not they agree. We should do something. Don't you think so?" Barbie asked Skipper.

Skipper was feeling confused. She agreed with everything Barbie had said. But she didn't want people to be angry at her. Was voting really that important? Besides, what could Skipper do about it? She was just *one person*.

Finally Skipper said, "All the things Miss Anthony talked about, you already do, Barbie. You have your own business. You take care of your own banking. And you're just as good at it as Mr. Kelvin is at the General Store."

"But Skipper," Barbie pointed out, "I can do those things only because I'm not married. And Mr. Kelvin can vote, and I can't. Remember when I suggested that Main Street be paved with stones so it would be easier to cross on rainy days? Every woman in town liked the idea. But most of the men thought it was a waste of money.

And because only men can vote, Main Street is still unpaved."

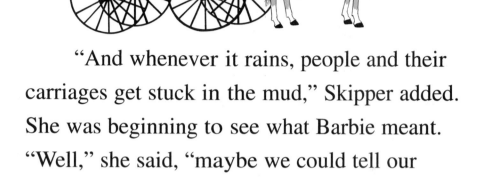

"And whenever it rains, people and their carriages get stuck in the mud," Skipper added. She was beginning to see what Barbie meant. "Well," she said, "maybe we could tell our customers about Miss Anthony's speech."

"That's a good idea," said Barbie. "And I have another idea, too. Here's my plan . . ."

At noon that day, Barbie closed the shoppe. She put on her favorite dress. Then she and Skipper went to Mr. Sims's newspaper office.

"Mr. Sims," Barbie said, "I'd like to write an article for the newspaper."

Mr. Sims clapped his hands. "That's wonderful! Our paper could use a good article on fashion. Maybe we could give *Godey's* some competition!" He looked over at Skipper. "And will you be doing the drawings?"

Barbie jumped in before Skipper could answer. "Actually, Mr. Sims, I'd like to do an article about Miss Anthony's speech. So Skipper's drawing would be of Miss Anthony."

Mr. Sims folded his arms. His smile disappeared. "Miss Roberts," he said, "I think you know how I feel about Miss Anthony. Now if you write a fashion article, I'll print that. Fashion," he said, nodding, "that's what's important to women."

Skipper's face flushed with anger. "Fashion is only one thing that's important to women," Skipper corrected. "And women already know about it. They *don't* know what Miss Anthony said in her speech the other night."

"And they don't need to," Mr. Sims answered briskly. "Voting is too difficult for women. They need to leave that up to men."

Before Skipper could argue, Barbie spoke up. "Mr. Sims," she said in a calm voice, "I thought that your newspaper covered all the important news in town. Miss Anthony is an important woman. There should be something in the paper about her, even if you disagree with her ideas."

"Susan B. Anthony is not worthy of a story. Besides," the editor added, "do you know what would happen if I printed a story about her? Every man in town would stop buying my paper."

"Well," Barbie said politely, "if she has that much power, she must be more important than you think."

Mr. Sims stood up and walked Barbie and Skipper to the door. "Ladies, I believe I know more than you do about the news. If you think you know better," he said to Barbie, "then maybe you should start your own paper." Mr. Sims closed the door behind them.

"Now what?" asked Skipper.

Barbie smiled. "Now we do just what he suggested."

Skipper was surprised. "Stay with fashion instead of reporting?"

Barbie shook her head. "No. Start our own newspaper!"

Chapter Four

That night, after closing the shoppe, Skipper and Barbie cleared the sewing table and sat down. Smoothing out a sheet of paper, Barbie wrote down everything she could remember about Miss Anthony's speech and visit. The shouts of the crowd and the words in Miss Anthony's speech became part of Barbie's story.

Skipper drew a picture of Miss Anthony sitting on the small stage, waiting to speak. She wanted people to see Susan B. Anthony just as she and Barbie had seen her. The older woman had worn a dark dress. But she had a red shawl over her shoulders. Her hair had been pulled back in a bun. Behind her glasses, Miss Anthony's eyes looked intelligent. Skipper drew a thoughtful expression on her face. Barbie was still writing when Skipper  finished. So Skipper began a second drawing of Mr. Sims. In it he was crumpling a Susan B. Anthony sign in his hands.

Barbie chuckled when she saw it. "Let's hold off on that one. But keep it. We may use it later." She tapped Skipper's drawing of Miss Anthony. "That's very good, Skipper. She didn't look like much of a troublemaker, did she?"

Skipper smiled. "No. And now everyone else will be able to see that, too."

The next morning, before they opened the shoppe, Barbie and Skipper took their story over to the place where *The Globe* was printed. The printer's eyes widened when he saw the drawing of Susan B. Anthony and read the story. "Of course I'll need to check with Mr. Sims first."

"This isn't for *The Globe,*" Barbie explained. "It's for me."

The printer lowered his voice. "It's just that *The Globe* is my biggest customer. If Mr. Sims doesn't like what I print, I could lose a lot of money." Raising his voice again, the printer said, "Please wait here."

Within minutes, the printer came back with Mr. Sims from next door.

"Miss Roberts," the editor began, "your writing is a nice little hobby, but you should keep it to yourself. This business will not be printing any stories about Susan B. Anthony." He glared at the printer. "Because if it does, *The Globe* will take its business elsewhere!"

The printer cleared his throat nervously.

He handed the story back to Barbie. "Sorry," he said. Then he hurried into his back room.

Mr. Sims smiled and bowed. "Good day, ladies," he said as he left.

Skipper and Barbie stepped outside. "Mr. Sims sure has a lot of power in this town," Skipper sighed.

"We'll just have to find another way to get this printed," Barbie told her.

As they stood outside, a horse and carriage slowly rolled past. They watched it stop in front of the blacksmith.

Skipper turned to her sister excitedly. "Barbie," she began, "do you remember what the blacksmith told us last week?"

Barbie snapped her fingers. "His friend just set up a printing shoppe in the next town! Good thinking, Skipper! Mr. Sims doesn't have any power over there. That printer could probably use some business." Barbie smiled down at their article. "We'll just stop by the stable and hitch up our carriage at noon. Then we'll take a ride over to that print shoppe."

The morning went quickly. Skipper and Barbie were attentive as usual to their customers. But both of them could hardly wait until noon. As soon as the town clock struck twelve, they put the Closed sign in the window and hurried over to the next town.

The two sisters showed the new printer their story. He let out a long, slow whistle. "You're sure going to raise a lot of fuss with this," he said.

"But you'll still print it, won't you?" Skipper asked.

"Yes, ma'am," the man chuckled, "that's my job. You can pick it up on Tuesday."

Four days later, the printer handed them the finished story.

"It's wonderful!" Barbie and Skipper cried.

The man smiled. "I just printed what you gave me."

"It just looks so much better in print," Skipper explained.

Barbie nodded. "It will look even better in our store's front window," she added.

As soon as Barbie and Skipper got back, Barbie put their story on display in the front window. Then she put a stack of copies on a table near the door. She also put out her copy of Miss Anthony's paper, *The Revolution.* Before long, a small group of people had gathered.

Barbie and Skipper's customers read while they were being fitted for new dresses. Some of them tucked copies of the story into their purses to read at home. Mrs. Steele snorted when she saw Barbie and Skipper's story. But Skipper saw her sneak a copy of it into her plain, gray handbag as she left the shoppe.

All of the women talked about the story,

even those who had been afraid to go to the speech. Barbie's customers thanked her for passing along the information.

Not everyone was happy about Barbie's news, though. Skipper found that out at Kelvin's General Store at the end of the week.

Mr. Kelvin seemed nervous as he handed Skipper her spools of thread. The two men playing checkers in the store seemed to be watching her. Then Skipper saw why. The newest edition of *The Globe* was on the counter. On the front page was a drawing of the dress shoppe with a paper in the window. But there was a big X drawn over it. Skipper's eyes moved to the headline. It said "Storefront News: Don't Read It!"

Chapter Five

"I can't believe Mr. Sims did this," Skipper sputtered as she rushed into the dress shoppe waving the paper.

Barbie sighed. "I'm not surprised. Let's see what it says." She began reading aloud. "'A certain woman with a Main Street business has taken up the cause of a known troublemaker. She is using her shoppe to fight for something that has no place in our town. Stop buying your dresses there! Show this woman that you want her out of the bad-news business. Let her get back to her dresses, where she belongs!'"

Barbie looked up and laughed. "That doesn't even make sense. How am I supposed to stay in the dress business if he's telling my customers to stay away?"

It didn't seem funny to Skipper, though. "What if people listen to him, Barbie?" she asked. "What if they stop coming here?"

Barbie looked up from the newspaper. "People will have to make up their own minds, Skipper. They can listen to others, or they can do what they believe is right."

The shoppe door opened, then shut with a bang. Mrs. Steele stood in the doorway, shaking *The Globe* at them. "This is **ridiculous**!" she said. "Does that Mr. Sims think I'm too stupid to make up my own mind?" She stomped over to the fitting area. "I believe you have a dress to finish for me." As Barbie brought out the dress, Mrs. Steele added, "I may not like what your Miss Anthony says. But I have a right to hear about it!"

Skipper was relieved.

Mrs. Steele was the first customer that day, but she wasn't the last. Other women came in. All of them made a point of thanking Barbie and Skipper for writing their story.

Barbie was pleased that her customers were standing by her and Skipper. But she still needed to face Mr. Sims. At noon, she and Skipper closed the shoppe again. Then they paid another visit to the newspaper office.

"Mr. Sims," Barbie said to the editor, "there was one thing you forgot to say in your article about me. I put my article in my window because you wouldn't print it in your paper. I'd like the chance to answer what you've said, in print."

Mr. Sims leaned his chair back. "Go right ahead," he told Barbie.

"We'd like you to print it in *your* paper, Mr. Sims," Skipper added.

The newspaper editor let his chair drop back

to the floor with a thud. "Absolutely not. That is final." He stood up behind his desk. "Thank you for visiting."

The sisters turned and walked back to their shoppe. There, they saw a crowd of curious people looking at their front-window story. "Well, Skipper," sighed Barbie, "I think we can use that drawing you did of Mr. Sims now."

That night, Barbie wrote a second story. She explained that *The Globe* would not print a story on Miss Anthony. If the town newspaper would not fully inform its readers, she told them, she would do it herself.

Skipper smiled as she read the story. "This is great, Barbie! There's just one thing missing. We need a name for the paper."

"How about *The Front Window*? That's where most people will read it," Barbie said with a laugh.

"That's perfect!" Skipper took out her pen

and ink. She carefully wrote *The Front Window* in bold letters over Barbie's story. "We should have a motto, too, like Miss Anthony's paper." After a moment, Skipper said, "How about A Look Outside?"

Barbie nodded. Skipper added the words under *The Front Window*.

The next morning, they took the second story over to the print shoppe. Early Tuesday morning, Barbie posted the new story in her store window. It was raining that day, so only a few people stopped outside to read it.

Mrs. Steele read it inside as Barbie fitted a dress for her. "This is all well and good," she said. "But if you want to report on something important, just take a look at the street out there! And look at my old skirt!" She pointed to the mud splattered on the gray material. "I've told Jonas Sims a hundred times to write about paving Main Street. Do you think he listens? No!

I think he has rocks in his head!"

After Mrs. Steele left, Barbie and Skipper looked out at Main Street. It was a muddy, soggy mess. A single horse-drawn carriage slowly made its way down the street. The horse's hooves sank in the mud with each step. There were no customers on Main Street, not even at Mr. Kelvin's store. "You know," said Barbie, "those paving stones aren't just important for keeping our skirts clean. When Main Street is muddy, most people don't leave their homes to shop. All the stores lose customers on a rainy day."

"And no customers means no money," added Skipper.

"Exactly," said Barbie.

So Barbie wrote her third story. The headline was "Rock Solid Business Sense." She even interviewed Mr. Kelvin. The storekeeper had to admit that business was terrible when it rained.

Skipper drew a picture of the Main Street businesses sinking in the mud.

This time when Barbie posted her story, a large crowd gathered to read it. Barbie's customers took copies of the story home to show their husbands.

Barbie's customers brought up another problem, too. They asked Barbie to write about the old schoolhouse. Its roof was leaking, and its floor was missing some boards. "The whole place is ready to fall down. We need a new schoolhouse," Barbie **quoted** one of the women.

Even more people read that story. Barbie started selling the paper at a little table just inside the shoppe. Barbie and Skipper could sometimes see Mr. Sims glaring at them from across the street, but it didn't bother them. Barbie's news got the townspeople talking and thinking. Women still couldn't vote. But they started telling their husbands how they felt about important issues.

One Thursday, *The Globe* printed a notice. A town meeting was going to be held the next night. Two votes would be taken at the meeting. One vote would be on paving Main Street. The other vote would be on building a new school.

"I guess Mr. Sims has learned that women are interested in more than fashion!" Skipper declared as she read the notice.

Barbie laughed and said, "Our work isn't done yet." Skipper noticed a twinkle in her eye. Barbie had a plan. She knew that Mr. Sims kept a strict printing schedule. No matter what happened at Friday's meeting, he didn't print his next paper until the following Thursday.

But Barbie was going to write an article about Friday's meeting just as soon as it ended. Barbie had asked her printer to do a rush printing job. She wanted to get the news out first.

On Friday night, Barbie and Skipper hurried

over to the meeting. Skipper looked around the hall. Almost every seat was taken. And Skipper was pleased to see almost as many women as men in the crowd.

"I don't see Mr. Sims," Skipper whispered.

"I guess he figures he'll just find out from someone else," replied Barbie.

There was an excited buzz in the hall as the mayor stepped onto the stage. People quieted down as he spoke about paving Main Street. As Barbie took notes, Skipper sketched a man with a beard speaking to the crowd.

Then it was time for the vote. Barbie squeezed Skipper's arm. The men voted yes! Everyone cheered.

The hall quieted down as the second vote began. Should they build a new school?

"All in favor?" said the mayor.

There were murmurs in the crowd. Barbie heard the phrases "a lot of money" and "not in such bad shape" from the men. But the women were whispering "Yes!" and "think of the children" to their husbands. When the vote was counted, the nays won. There would be no new school.

"Well, that's all the business tonight," the mayor said.

Then Skipper saw Mrs. Steele nudging her husband out of his seat. Skipper leaned forward. She had never heard *Mr.* Steele speak. "I have a suggestion," he said, twisting his hat in his hands. "If we're not going to build a new school, why don't we fix up the old one? We need new floors and a new roof." He was about to sit down, but his wife pushed him back up.

"Does anyone second that motion?" asked the mayor.

There was a pause, and then Mr. Kelvin

called out, "Second!"

"All those in favor?" asked the mayor.

"Yes!" came the answer loud and clear. Almost everyone voted to fix the school!

As the crowd cheered again, Barbie and Skipper ran back to the dress shoppe. Barbie wrote the story, and Skipper finished her drawings. It was very late by the time they finished.

Early the next morning, they took the story and drawings over to the print shoppe. And on Monday morning, Barbie and Skipper posted the paper in their front window. They had beaten Mr. Sims to the story! Barbie smiled proudly as she stood outside and looked at the story in the window. Then she laughed. Next to the story, Skipper was putting up a sign: "You Read It Here First!"

Chapter Six

After that, Barbie and Skipper spent more and more time working on the newspaper. The dressmaking shoppe stayed in the front of the store. The back room was filled with two desks, notebooks, and drawings as *The Front Window* grew into a full-scale newspaper. Barbie's shoppe became the center of town news.

One morning as Skipper came to the shoppe, she saw a newspaper crumpled up near the door. Curious, she picked it up and smoothed it out. It was a copy of *The Globe.* Skipper laughed and crumpled the paper back up . . .

*****

Just then, Skipper sat up suddenly as a beeping sound woke her up. "Whew," she yawned. "That was some dream!" She rubbed her eyes and looked at the glowing numbers on her watch. It was four-thirty! The library would close soon. Skipper hurried over to the microfilm file cabinet. She couldn't find any *Front Window* reels after 1873.

On a hunch, Skipper pulled out a *Globe* reel from 1874. She quickly put the reel on the machine and searched the newspaper. She smiled at what she saw. By 1874, Mr. Sims was gone. The new editor in chief of *The Globe* was a woman. She was the same woman who had owned the dress shop and started *The Front Window.*

Skipper printed out some pages and thanked the librarian on her way out. That night, Skipper arrived early for the speech. She was thrilled to see reporters from all over the state in the audience.

She even noticed that the reporter from *The Globe* was a woman. She smiled. What would Mr. Sims have said all those years ago?

Skipper tested her tape recorder to make sure that it was working. She didn't want to miss a word. The speaker didn't disappoint her. She talked about how hard women had worked and how much progress they had made.

"We should be proud of our successes," she finished. "But we must never forget what it was like not to have a voice in the world. We must always speak for those women and men who do not have a voice."

At home later, Skipper played back those words again and took notes. Then she wrote her story. It was about two newspapers: One that wanted to give women a voice, and another that wanted to stop them. It was about how earlier women cleared a path for today's women in the news and in their lives.

Monday afternoon, Skipper waited as her adviser read her story. "This is great, Skipper! I had never heard of *The Front Window,*" Becky said. "In fact, once we print your story, I'm going to send a copy over to *The Globe.*" She smiled. "I think Nancy Williams, the editor in chief, will like it."

Skipper smiled. She didn't even mind when Kevin told her how great the 'N Pink concert had been. Skipper had forgotten all about it.

Two days later, Becky called Skipper into the newspaper office. She held up a copy of *The Globe.* "Nancy Williams definitely liked your story," she said. Becky pointed to the front page of *The Globe.* There was Skipper's story for everyone to read! The title of her story was simply "Women in the News—From Fashion to Front Page."

The Revolution.

PRINCIPLE, NOT POLICY: JUSTICE, NOT FAVORS.

NEW YORK, WEDNESDAY, JANUARY 8, 1868.

VOL. I.—NO. 1.

The Revolution;

THE ORGAN OF THE

NATIONAL PARTY OF NEW AMERICA.

POLICY—INDIVIDUAL RIGHTS AND
SIBILITIES.

WILL OCATE:

Educat frage, Irrespective of
Pay to women for Equal Work;
olition of Standing Armies and
with Politicians—Up with the

ought; Prouder Idea;
Party; Love to Man

Reform; Practical
not Fiction; Vic-
oholic Drinks or Medi-
ous Personalities and In-
Advertisements, so common
us Newspapers.

Revolution proposes a new Commercial and
cial Policy. America no longer led by Europe.
d live our Cotton and Corn for sale. Greenbacks for
money. All American System of Finance, American
Products and Labor Free. Foreign Manufactures Pro-
ibited. Open doors to Artisans and Immigrants.
Atlantic and Pacific Oceans for American Steamships
and Shipping; or American goods in American bottoms.
New York the Financial Centre of the World. Wall
Street emancipated from Bank of England, or American
Cash for American Bills. The Credit Foncier and
Mobilier System, or Capital Mobilized to Re-
and our Mining Interests, and to
Ocean to Ocean, from Omaha
ed Labor, more Cotton,
foreigners at the
Citizens

KANSAS.

The question of the enfranchisement of woman has already passed the court of moral dis-
cussion, and is now fairly ushered into the arena
of politics, where it must remain a fixed ele-
ment of debate, until party necessity shall com-
pel its success.

With 9,000 votes in Kansas, one-third the
entire vote, every politician must see that
the friends of "woman's suffrage" hold the
balance of power in that State to-day. And
those 9,000 votes represent a principle deep in
the hearts of the people, for this triumph was
secured without money, without a press, without a party. With these instrumentalities now
fast coming to us on all sides, the victory in
every State of the Union. Kansas already leads
the world in her legislation for woman on ques-
tions of property, education, wages, marriage
and divorce. Her best unive

on
oi
an
sen
fem
sto
of t
the t
of wo
and o
pulpit
positio
Kansas
Robins
every d
suffrag
governm
"white
Kansas e
ing politi
that State,
eyes to th
women, the
tory, does
al as

ence outside as well as
bined might have mad
a small one, had not
into the State two w
galvanized the De
securing 9,000 vot
claim that we a
for this vot
republican
largest v
Leavenwo
largest v

In say
vote tak
who lab
All pr
Susan
Judg
hard
stre

The Power of the Ballot

Wannamaker's Barn
Wednesday Eve, March 3d, 1870

AT 8 O'CLOCK

at Kelvin's General S...
It comes in handy ...
mistakes.

March 10, 1870

My, how things have changed ...ce that fateful day when I ...ard Miss Anthony speak. Printing ...at first story has changed my life. ...wonder if that's how Miss Anthony ...nd Mrs. Stanton felt after publishing ...their first issue of *The Revolution?* It might hurt my business, but I have to do what I believe is right. So, if *The Globe* won't print differing points of view, then someone else has to — even if that someone is me! I don't know what's going to happen next, but it's exciting to have people sit up and listen.

I think Skipper did a terrific job on her sketch of Miss Anthony. I've asked her if I could keep her first draft for my journal.

I bought a little scratch knife

Roberts' Dress Shoppe				June-July,
Date	Item	Debit/ Credit	Income/ Expense	
June 02	6½ yds. - muslin (8¢/yd.)		52	
	4 spools - blue cotton (5¢ ea.)	D	0	
na	1 ³/₁₂ hooks & eyes		0	
	calico		90	
			$ .15	

July 9, 1870

<u>The Front Window</u> actually
made a profit — one whole dollar!
Even though I'm staring at the
coin right now, I still can't
believe it. When I started the
newspaper, I never expected to
turn it into a business of its own.
I'm so excited!

On the other hand, with two
businesses to run, the dress shoppe
is becoming rather cluttered. I dread
the day someone knocks over an inkwell
onto a bolt of fabric. It's difficult
to keep everything in its place.

But I wouldn't have it any other way.

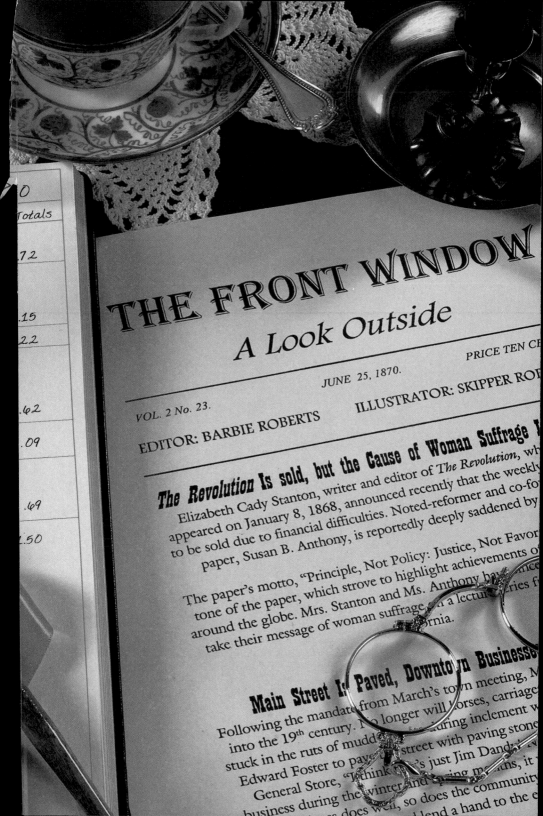

	Totals
0	
	7.2
	.15
	2.2
	.62
	.09
	.69
	.50

THE FRONT WINDOW

A Look Outside

PRICE TEN C

JUNE 25, 1870.

VOL. 2 No. 23.

ILLUSTRATOR: SKIPPER ROI

EDITOR: BARBIE ROBERTS

The Revolution Is sold, but the Cause of Woman Suffrage I

Elizabeth Cady Stanton, writer and editor of *The Revolution*, wh appeared on January 8, 1868, announced recently that the weekly to be sold due to financial difficulties. Noted-reformer and co-fo paper, Susan B. Anthony, is reportedly deeply saddened by

The paper's motto, "Principle, Not Policy: Justice, Not Favor tone of the paper, which strove to highlight achievements of around the globe. Mrs. Stanton and Ms. Anthony ba nce take their message of woman suffrage n a lectu ries fi rnia.

Main Street I Paved, Downto n Businesse

Following the mandat from March's to n meeting, M into the 19th century. o longer will orses, carriage stuck in the ruts of mudd street with paving stone Edward Foster to pa just Jim Dand General Store, " think s ng m hs, it business during the winter and does w , so does the community d lend a hand to the

Lucy Stone

Sojourner Truth

Julia Ward Howe

November 15, 1870

I've been wanting to write about woman suffrage in our paper for a while. And now my story is finally taking shape. Yesterday, I received a photo of Miss Anthony and Mrs. Stanton in the mail. Now I have six women to write about in The Front Window. Skipper is going to use the photos to draw her illustrations for the story. The information that I requested from The New York Herald arrived today. I requested two stories on the annual meeting of the American Equal Rights Association last week.

Elizabeth Cady Stanton/Susan B. Anthony

LC-USZ61-791 DLC

I'm calling the story "The Voices of Change." Julia Ward Howe, Sojourner (SOH-jer-ner) Truth, Lucy Stone, Lucretia (LOO-kree-shuh) Mott... those are just a few of the people who are fighting to improve the lives of women. I believe that their efforts will have a great impact on future generations of women everywhere.

I still have quite a bit of work left to do on the story. But I don't mind. I love what I'm doing. More important, I really feel that I, too, can help make a difference — however small — in people's lives.

LC-USZ62-42559 DLC

Lucretia Mott

Dear Miss Roberts,

I am quite pleased with my
new dress from Roberts' Dress
Shoppe. Perhaps it has a bit
too much blue for my taste,
but it fits properly.

I am truly impressed, however,
with the little paper you and
your sister have been printing.

I have just one thing to say:
It's about time. There is no
reason whatsoever why we
women should wait for our
men to tell us what is
happening. And for that,
Miss Roberts, I am grateful.

Yours truly,
Mrs. Jacob Steele

November 26, 1871

I just opened a drawer and found the
most wonderful thing. It's the drawing
Skipper did of the dress I wore to Miss
Anthony's speech. I'm always amazed at
how talented my sister is. The colors and
fabrics she chose for the dress were
lovely. I will keep a few fabric swatches
in my journal to remind me.

We kept the dress displayed in
the store for a long time afterward.
It's actually become quite a popular
style with customers. And now, more
than one year later, it still reminds
me of that eventful night.

In that same drawer, I
also found a note from one
of our most loyal customers
Mrs. Steel. It, too, holds a
special place in my heart.

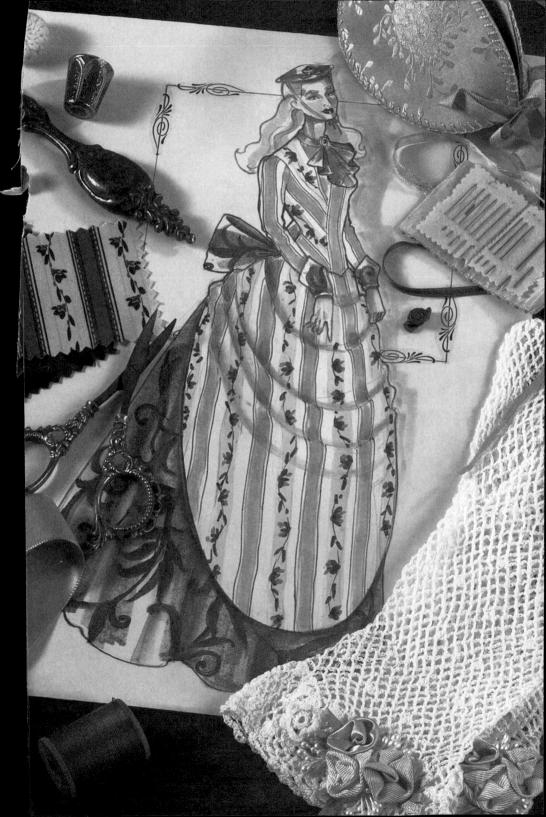